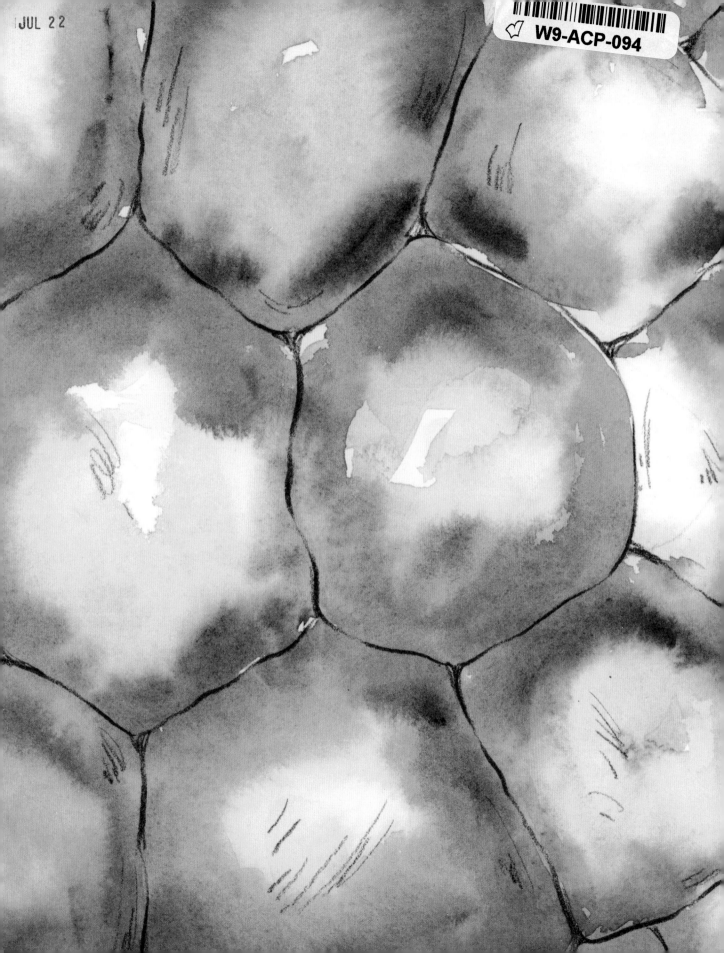

RODNEY
WAS A TORTOISE

written by NAN FORLER
illustrated by YONG LING KANG

tundra

RODNEY was an old pal.

He was older than Bernadette,
older than her dad, even older
than Great-Aunt Clara.

"He is practically prehistoric!"
Bernadette told her class on Pet Day.

Day after day,
   year after year,
      Rodney was there,
      loyal and true.

Together, Rodney and Bernadette
played Go Fish and Crokinole.
(Bernadette took Rodney's turns for him.)

They had contests to see who could
stare the longest without laughing.
(Rodney always won.)

When Bernadette dressed up as queen of the castle,
she made a tiny crown for Rodney.

It took almost all day for Rodney to look up,
but she could tell he loved it.

While Bernadette gobbled up raspberry scones
and slurped lemonade, Rodney munched on a piece
of lettuce VERRRRRRY SLOOOOOWLY.

At bedtime, Bernadette read stories of creatures
from creeks and forests and did all the voices,
as Rodney snoozed in the tank beside her.

When she said the tortoise lines,
she was sure she caught him smiling.

Each night, Bernadette stared into the tank as she fell asleep. Rodney was there, snug on his rock.

"You're a real old pal, Rodney," she'd say.

As the seasons passed,
sleepy old Rodney seemed to move
slower
and slower,
and slower,

until finally one day,
Rodney moved so slowly

that he stopped.

Bernadette watched and waited
and waited and watched,
but still, Rodney did not move.

"Maybe he's just holding his breath to be funny,"
Bernadette suggested. "He's such a joker."

"Bernadette," said her mother,
"I think Rodney is dead."

They put Rodney in a shoe box
and buried him near the lettuce plants he loved.

They all said things they had learned from Rodney.

Be a pal.

Slow down.

Chew your food.

Enjoy each piece of lettuce.

Bernadette sang a
goodbye song.

The next day, Bernadette was slow getting ready
and took a long time walking to school.

All she could think about was Rodney.

RODNEY, RODNEY, RODNEY

But no one at school talked about Rodney.

"My piano teacher
got a new cat,"
said Naya.

"Margaret's
brother broke his
toe," said Elliot.

"It's my birthday next May,"
said Sofia.

Bernadette pulled her turtleneck
up around her ears.

"Rodney died," she whispered.

No one seemed to hear.

At home, Bernadette still set a place for Rodney at the table and read stories to his empty tank at night.

She sat on her bed with a hurt deep down in her stomach that even soda crackers and ginger ale couldn't fix.

And so, each morning,
Bernadette put on her protective shell,
and lumbered to school.

She sat,
huddled on a rock,
quiet and still.

The other kids ran and whirled past her
as though Rodney had never existed.

She crawled deeper and deeper into her shell
until all of Bernadette seemed to have disappeared.

RODNEY, RODNEY, RODNEY

It was Amar who spotted Bernadette,
tucked away in her green coat.
He came and sat on the rock beside her.

"You must be very sad about Rodney," he finally said.

Bernadette slowly lifted her head.

"I am," she said, quietly.

"I remember when you brought him to
school for Pet Day. He was asleep, but
he looked like he was smiling."

"Yeah, he was a real old pal."

"I used to have a budgie
named Samuel," said Amar.

"Amar, do you like Crokinole?"

For my beloved Coatsie family and their animals,
past, present and future. — NF

To Irene and Charlene, for the fun times we spent
with Sasha and Mindy! — YLK

Text copyright © 2022 by Nan Forler
Illustrations copyright © 2022 by Yong Ling Kang

Tundra Books, an imprint of Penguin Random House Canada Young Readers,
a division of Penguin Random House of Canada Limited

Library and Archives Canada Cataloguing in Publication

Title: Rodney was a tortoise / Nan Forler, Yong Ling Kang.
Names: Forler, Nan, author. | Kang, Yong Ling, illustrator.
Identifiers: Canadiana (print) 20200380397 | Canadiana (ebook) 20200380427
ISBN 9780735266629 (hardcover) | ISBN 9780735266636 (EPUB)
Subjects: LCGFT: Picture books.
Classification: LCC PS8611.O76 R63 2022 | DDC jC813/.6—dc23

Published simultaneously in the United States of America by Tundra Books of Northern New York,
an imprint of Penguin Random House Canada Young Readers,
a division of Penguin Random House of Canada Limited

Library of Congress Control Number: 2020948995

Edited by Debbie Rogosin and Elizabeth Kribs
Designed by John Martz
The artwork in this book was created with watercolor and pencil.
The text was set in Stone Serif.

Printed in China

www.penguinrandomhouse.ca

1 2 3 4 5   26 25 24 23 22

Penguin
Random House
tundra | TUNDRA BOOKS

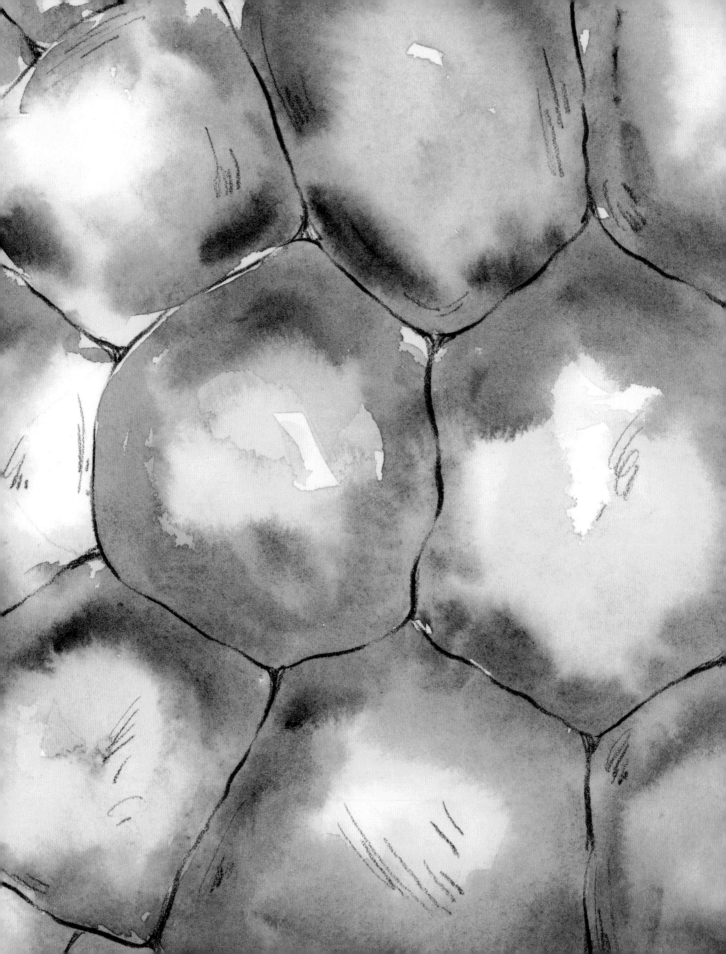